OLiViA'S Secret Scribbles

Super Science Stars

Kane Miller
A DIVISION OF EDC PUBLISHING

D0616404

For Charli Hatch, Super Science Star!—M.C.

For Bridget, Marty, Lachie and Clancy.—D.M.

First American Edition 2021
Kane Miller, A Division of EDC Publishing

Text copyright © Meredith Costain, 2019
Illustrations copyright © Danielle McDonald, 2019

First published by Scholastic Australia Pty Limited in 2019.
This edition published under license from Scholastic Australia Pty Limited.

Library of Congress Control Number: 2020949893

Printed and bound in the United States of America

1 2 3 4 5 6 7 8 9 10

ISBN: 978-1-68464-300-4

OLIVIA'S BIG BOOK of PRIVATE SECRETS

DO NOT OPEN!

GO AWAY!

KEEP OUT

(This means you, Max, and mainly you, Ella!!!)

Super Science Tuesday

I am SO excited. Next week at school we
are having a

Every class will make their own
experiments for it. And there's going to be
a prize for the best one.

And guess who the judges are going to be?
Real scientists! I really, really, really
want to win.

I ♥ science!

I am making lots of fun science projects right here in my bedroom already.

This is a special glittery lava lamp I made to put on my bedside table. It was super easy to make. (I "borrowed" the glitter for it from Ella's Big Box of Craft Supplies. I don't think she's noticed—yet. ☺)

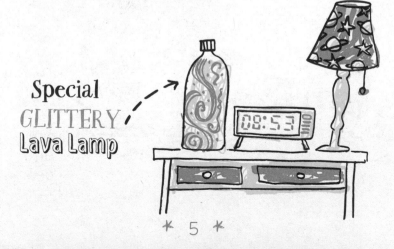

Special
GLITTERY
Lava Lamp

This is my big bowl of slippery, stretchy slime. I love squishing it around in my hands.

This is my **magnificent mold**. It's a little bit smelly. I have to keep it under my bed in case Mom finds it and makes me throw it out.

My magnificent mold

Salad Sandwich

CHEESE

Yogurt

watermelon

chocolate chip cookie

This is my potted plant project to see if plants can grow without sunlight or water.

Potted
Plant
  project

The answer is no. No, they can't. ☹
(Sorry, Mom!)

Our teacher, Mr. Platt, divided our class into four groups.

MR. PLATT

Our group is the best. It has lots of my friends in it.

HARRY   NiCO   ME   MatiLDa (My ♥BFF)

Ava   Daisy

The first thing we did was decide what to call ourselves. Here are some names we came up with.

Ava: We ♥ Science

HARRY: Brainy Superheroes

Matilda: The Science Detectives

OLIVIA: Crazy Comets

Everyone thought **MY** name was the **BEST**. ☺

We were just drawing some little
pictures of comets when there
was a knock on the door.

Mrs. Gupta, the lady
from the office,
came into our room.
And standing next to
her was a girl with
bouncy hair.

Her name is Bethany.
And guess what? She's
going to be in our class!

Mr. Platt asked Matilda and me to make some room at our table so Bethany could join our group.

At first I didn't want her to. I whispered to Matilda that we already have a good group. We don't need any more people in it.

Especially new ones we don't know anything about.

But then Matilda reminded me that she was the new girl once too. And it can be a bit scary when you don't have any friends to sit next to or play with. So we should all give Bethany a big welcome.

So that's what I did.

Hi, Bethany! Come and sit next to me!

Bethany bounced straight over. But she didn't sit next to me. She sat next to Harry instead.

"What's this group for?" she asked him.

"The school science fair," said Harry. "We're thinking up projects and a group name."

"Cool," said Bethany. "I LOVE science fairs. At my old school, my group won the top prize every year."

"Cool," said Harry. "Maybe our group will win this time too."

"Ours is the best group out of the whole class," added Nico. "We're called the Crazy Comets."

I showed her some of the little pictures we'd been drawing to go with our name.

But Bethany just wrinkled up her nose. "Crazy Comets is a silly name," she said. "I think we should call ourselves the ☆SUPER Science* STARS* instead. That's what our group was called when we won the top prize."

And guess what? Everyone thought Super Science Stars was a much better prizewinning name too. (Except for Matilda and me.)

So now that's what we're called.

livia

After dinner

At dinner tonight, I told everyone I had interesting news.

Ella: I already know what it is.

Me: No, you don't.

Ella: Yes, I do.

Me: Don't.

Ella: Do. Your class is going to make stuff for the science fair.

Me: How did you know that?

Ella: The whole school is doing the science fair! Everyone's class is going to be in it. Hehehe.

Hmmmph. Ella thinks she is soooo smart.

Hmmmph

Me: Oh right. I forgot. Well anyway, that's only half my interesting news. You'll never be able to guess what else happened today.

Bet I can.

Ella: Bet I can.

Me: Can't.

Can't.

Ella: Can.

Can.

Mom: Ella! Olivia! Stop arguing and eat your vegetables.

Me: 😣😣😣 (I hate vegetables. Especially broccoli. YUCK.)

Then Dad asked me what the second half of the interesting news was. But I didn't feel like telling them about Bethany anymore. Not after Ella spoiled my science fair story.

So I didn't.

I made a Christmas tree out of all my

vegetables instead. With a broccoli star on the top. ☺

livia

Later that night

I've just had a super-amazing idea for our project for the science fair!
It's superspecial. So superspecial I

bet no one in our school has ever done a project like it before.

Not even Bethany.

The judges are going to ♥ it. It's going to win the top prize for sure!

I can't wait for school tomorrow so I can tell everyone in our group what it is!

livia

Ideas Wednesday

I told Matilda all about my super—amazing idea on the way to school.

Matilda thought it was an excellent idea too. She said everyone in our group will love it!

As soon as we arrived I raced over to our special part of the playground, near the big tree. Ava and Daisy were already there. They were talking to Harry and Nico about the science fair.

Matilda ME AVA Daisy Nico HARRY

I was just about to tell them all my amazing idea when Bethany turned up.

And guess what she was holding?

Matching T-shirts with our new group name on the front.

T-shirts

Bethany gave everyone a T-shirt.

"Wow, thanks, Bethany!" Matilda said. Then she nudged my arm.

"Thanks, Bethany," I mumbled. (Why didn't I think of making cool T-shirts?!)

The bell rang and we all trooped off to our classroom.

When the time came for our science fair group meeting, we all put our new T-shirts on over the top of our school uniforms.

Everyone else in our class thought our new
T-shirts were awesome.

I patted one of the twinkly stars on the front of my top. I guess Bethany's T-shirts are OK. And they match our group name really well. (Though I still think my Crazy Comets name is better.)

Mr. Platt came over to our table.

"Great shirts, Super Science Stars," he said. "Where did you get them from?"

"Bethany gave them to us," Ava told him.

"Great work, Bethany,"
said Mr. Platt.

Bethany beamed. "My mom got them
printed last night. My group always had
special T—shirts at my last school. And we
always won the top prize."

Mr. Platt looked super impressed. "Has
your group decided what you're going to do
for this year's science fair yet?"

"Not yet," said Bethany, shaking
her head so that her bouncy
curls jumped up and down.

"But I've got some really, really good ideas," she grinned.

"I've got some really good ideas too," I reminded everyone.

Mr. Platt smiled at me. "I can't wait to see what you all come up with," he said. Then he moved on to the next group.

Everyone had a turn saying their favorite idea. Matilda wrote them all down on a big sheet of paper.

Harry wanted us all to make different kinds of paper planes. Then we would test them out to see which ones fly for the longest.

Cheetah

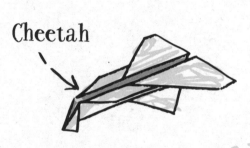

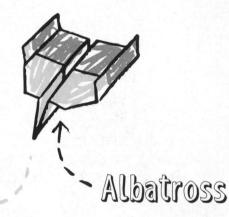

Albatross

THE JET Fighter

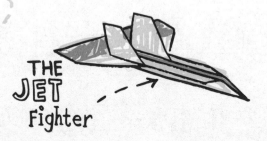

Ava wanted to do a jump rope test to see which length of rope is the best for jumping really fast. She wants to break the jump rope world record!

SHORT   Medium   LONG

World INTER-SCHOOL
JUMP ROPE CHAMPIONSHIPS

WORLD RECORD =

108 JUMPS in 30 SECONDS

Daisy wanted to build a rocket ship that will travel to Mars! With sleeping capsules for all her pets.

Matilda wanted to build little robots that can chase each other around the room.

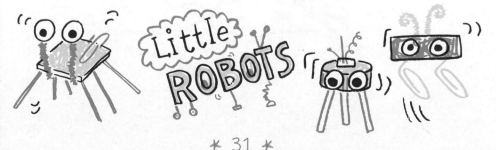

Nico wanted to try
all the chocolate
bars in the world
to see which one
tastes the best.

chocolate
BARS

I waited . . .

and waited . . .

and waited . . .

until . . .

finally, it was my turn.

CROSSED
fingers
and toes!

I took a deep breath
and crossed my fingers
and toes.

And then I said my brilliant idea.

Me: I think we should make a . . .

TIME Machine!

YES!

Matilda: Yes!

Nico: Cool!

Harry: Awesome!

Ava: Brilliant!

Bethany: A what?

Me: A time machine. So we can travel back in time.

Matilda: Or into the future.

Nico: Epic! I want to see the dinosaurs!

Harry: And Stone Age people!

Daisy: And space-age people! With space-age pets!

Ava: And robots that do your homework for you!

Nico: And make you snacks whenever you want them!

But Bethany didn't think my idea was very brilliant at all. ☹

Bethany: But time machines  don't even exist in real life, do they?

Me: Yes, they do!

Bethany: Aren't they just made-up things in stories?

Matilda: Olivia's time machine  is real. I've seen it.

Harry: Have you **really** got a time machine, Olivia?

So I told them all about the special machine I'm building in my bedroom. And how I only need a few more parts for it. And how they could be part of the **best science fair project ever** by helping me to finish it off.

We could all travel through time together. And write down all the exciting stuff we see in our science fair notebooks!

We might even win a **world-famous superspecial top science prize** for our project. And get in all the history books.

Or on TV!

But Bethany **still** didn't think time machines were real. And then my friends all started changing their minds about doing my idea. Even Matilda. ☹

Bethany: But how are you going to make it fly?

Harry: Yeah, how?

Ava: What if it breaks down halfway through a trip, and we get stuck in the Stone Age?

Daisy: And get eaten by saber-toothed tigers?

Matilda: What if we're all too heavy for it? And it never even leaves the ground?

Nico: I don't think it's going to work. Let's do something else.

It's so not fair. Everyone
agreed my science fair
project idea was super
amazing. And now nobody
wants to do it.

And it's all Bethany's
fault.

She's just a big bossy boots.

livia

A bit later . . .

Oops! I forgot to write the most important part.

There was still one member of our group who had to tell their best idea. Bethany.

She wanted to do an experiment with eggs she saw on TV. You have to put them in jars with different kinds of liquids in them.

Eggs→

OiL vinegar

WATER

She said one of these liquids will make an
egg's shell disappear into nothing.

Just like that!

And then the egg will be super bouncy!
Even though it's not cooked!

Bethany made it all sound really exciting. And also easy peasy to do. She said it would be much easier than building a rocket ship or traveling in a made-up time machine or finding every chocolate bar in the world.

And everyone (except me and Matilda) said:

So, then we had a vote to see which project we were going to do.

And guess which project got the most votes?

SUPER SCIENCE STARS
GROUP PROJECT

1. Paper planes test
2. Jump rope test
3. Rocket to Mars
4. Racing robots ✓
5. Chocolate bar tasting ✓
6. Time machine ✓
7. Bouncy egg ✓✓✓✓

Olivia

A bit later after that . . .

Only one person voted for my amazing time-machine project. It was probably Matilda, being a true best friend. (I'm the one who voted for her racing robots.)

My time machine took me hours and hours to make. I used lots of stuff for it from around our house. This is what it looks like.

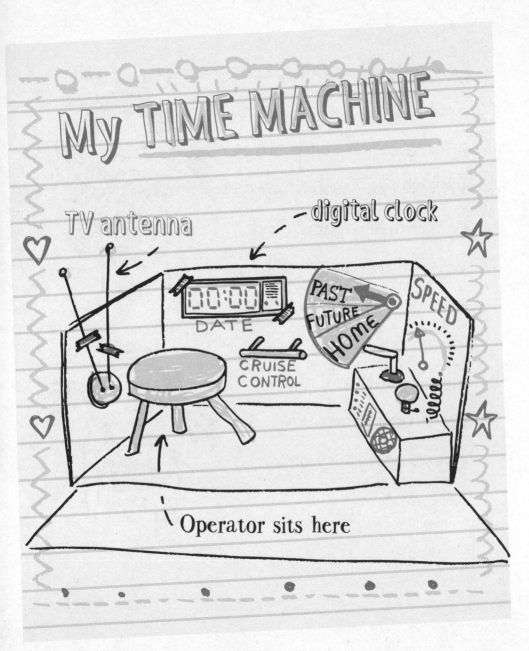

But what if it does break
down when we're in the
middle of the Stone Age?
Oops! How would we get
back home again? And
what if it isn't strong
enough to carry us all?

Maybe Bethany is right.
My time machine is
never going to work.
☹☹☹

But maybe her bouncy eggs experiment will work. I guess it might even be fun!

Olivia

Thrilling Thursday

Today everyone started working on their group projects for the science fair.

Sage and Samira's group are going to make a **rainbow** using a mirror, a piece of paper, a flashlight, and a tub of water.

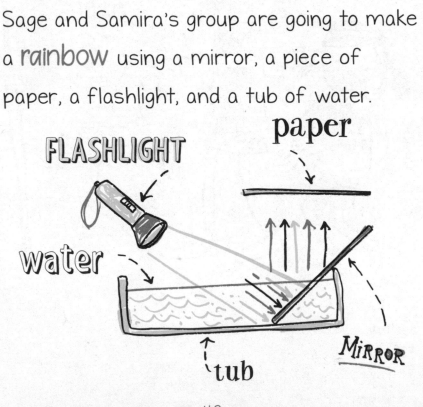

FLASHLIGHT

paper

water

tub

MiRRoR

Milo and Mehmet's group are dressing up like ducks with flippers for feet to see if it helps them to swim faster. They're going to make a video of their results at the swimming pool to show at the fair.

MiLo

Mehmet

stopwatch

FLiPPeRS

And Jamila and Ivy's group are going to make a balloon that doesn't pop, even if you push a pointy stick through it!

This is what it's going to look like.

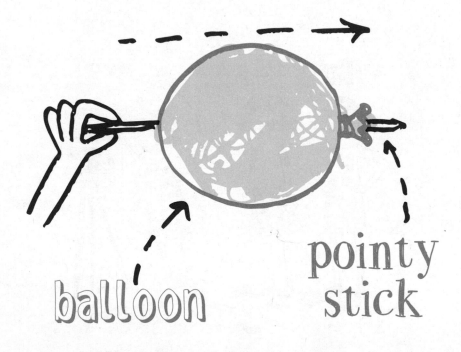

balloon

pointy stick

But nobody believes they can do it.

We put all the things we needed for our bouncing egg experiment on a table at the back of the room.

Pitcher OF WATER

Vinegar

Oil

EGGS

GLASS JARS

Harry poured a different liquid into each jar. Then Daisy carefully dropped in an egg.

And guess what?

One of the jars started to fill up with
teeny tiny bubbles, all around the egg!

Teeny TINY
BUBBLES

Bethany said we have to wait until
tomorrow to see what happens next.

But I don't think I can wait!

Olivia

Stinky Friday

Matilda and I couldn't wait to get to school today to see what had happened inside the jars!

As soon as the bell rang, we lined up
outside our classroom. Then we peered
through the window, trying to see if the
eggs had changed.

Finally, Mr. Platt let us all in. We raced over
to our experiment table. Bethany and the
rest of our group came too.

We took the eggs out of their jars with a spoon, one by one, and put them on a plate.

The first egg looked exactly the same.

So did the second egg.

But the third egg looked . . . disgusting!

Matilda poked it with her finger.

"Eww," she said. "It's all slimy and squishy."

Harry poked it too. "Hey," he said. "The shell's all gone!"

"Yeah!" said Nico. "The vinegar must have eaten it!"

We all stared at the egg. It was true. The shell had completely vanished!

POOF!!!

Just like Bethany said it would.

But there was another BIG problem.

The egg was now really stinky!!! Plus Bethany said the egg she had used was a really old one. Uh-oh!

Bethany picked up the squishy egg.

"Now we have to make it bounce," she said, smiling bravely. "Like the people in the experiment on TV did. Who wants to have the first turn?"

So Bethany did it herself. She held the smelly egg just above the plate. Then she gently dropped it.

BOING! The
egg bounced a
couple of times,
then stopped.

"That looks fun!" said
Daisy. She picked up
the egg and held it up
a little bit higher. Then
she dropped it.

The egg bounced around again, a little bit
more this time.

"Give me a turn!" said Nico, pushing forward.

He picked up the egg and held it up really high. Higher than his head!

Then he dropped it on the floor.

The rubbery egg broke open. Stinky, slimy eggy bits went everywhere!

"PEE-YEW!" screeched the other kids in our class. Then they ran to the other end of our classroom, with their hands over their mouths. Mr. Platt opened all the windows. And Tommy was sick. All over Ari's new shoes.

Nico: Oops!

Ava: That's disgusting!

Matilda: Eww.

Daisy: We can't do it. What if it makes the special science judges sick too?

Harry: Yeah. We'll never win the top prize now. ☹☹☹

Bethany: I guess we'll just have to do something else.

It was a  **DISASTER!**

Bethany looked really, really, **really** sad. Even her hair looked sad.

So we all gave her a . . .

BIG GROUP HUG.

Then we had a big meeting about a new project for the fair. Everyone had lots of ideas. But we couldn't agree about which one to choose.

So we decided we'd all have a big think about new ideas over the weekend. And start again on Monday.

But guess what?

We're not the only group in our class with a problem.

Jamila

Ivy

Jamila and Ivy's group have one too!

Every time they push the pointy stick into the balloon, it pops! And then the balloon flies around the room! Just like a big rubbery bat.

 Looks like **both** our groups need to come up with new ideas over the weekend.

But the science fair is only a few days away. We'll need to think **FAST!**

😞livia

Super Science Saturday

Matilda came over today so we could think up some extra-special new ideas for the science fair.

We found a comfy spot in the backyard
and flicked through My BIG BOOK OF
SUPER-AMAZING SCIENCE EXPERIMENTS!

Matilda

ME

Donkey

"This one looks awesome," said Matilda. "We
could make our own fossils."

"Fossils take gazillions of years to make," I reminded her. "And the science fair is this Wednesday!"

fossils

"Oh yeah," said Matilda. "Hmmm."

I turned the page. "What about a snail race?" I said. "You put one snail on a smooth path and another one on lumpy old dirt. And then you find out which path makes them go the fastest."

SNAIL RACE

Matilda wrinkled up her nose. "Eww. Snails are slimy and disgusting. Even more slimy and disgusting than stinky eggs."

☹☹☹ I ♥ snails. And so does my little brother, Max.

We were just about to give up when I found the PERFECT experiment for our group.

An exploding volcano!

And it was easy peasy to make!

YES!

I got so excited about our new idea that the hammock tipped over and we all fell out.

THUMP!

MROWWWR!

Then we went back inside
and collected the things
we needed for our volcano
from my experiment
cupboard.

brown
modeling
clay

PLASTiC
BOTTLE

We put the bottle on an old breadboard
we found in the kitchen. Then we pushed
and pulled the clay around it until it looked
exactly like a volcano!

And then guess who came snooping around?

My big sister, Ella, and her BFF, Zoe.

"What's that supposed to be?" Ella said, poking one of the sides.

"It's a volcano," I said proudly. "For the science fair. We're going to pour some special scientific stuff into it to make it explode."

"It looks just like a big pile of horse poop," said Ella.

"Or elephant poop," said Zoe.

"No, wait . . . dinosaur poop. Hehehe." Ella couldn't stop laughing.

Ella went out into the yard and came back with some pebbles and twigs. Then she showed me how to use them to make a better shape.

Matilda took lots of photos of our new and improved volcano. I can't wait to show them to our group at school on Monday. And then we can all start making our new volcano together!

Our super exploding volcano is going to be the best thing in the science fair. We're going to win the top prize for sure!

🙂livia

Super Sunday

Today was the best day ever. Matilda and I played soccer in the park with Mom and Max and Bob.

Dad made us
spaghetti and
meatballs for
lunch. Yum!

Spaghetti and
meatballs

Ella showed me some more cool ways to
decorate my volcano.

Glitter

ELLA'S BIG BOX of CRAFT STUFF

DO NOT TOUCH (EVER) WITHOUT MY PERMISSION

Then we all cuddled up on the couch together and watched old volcano movies.

Super VOLCANO DISASTER MOVIE

It was a perfect day. And tomorrow is going to be even better when I tell everyone about my idea! ☺☺☺

☺livia

Marvelous Monday

As soon as the bell rang I raced into our classroom. I was bursting to tell everyone about my super exploding–volcano project idea!

PHOTOS

But guess what?

Jamila and Ivy's group is making an exploding volcano for the science fair too! And they already started theirs over the weekend!

It looks really good.

OH NO!!

It's so not fair.
☹☹☹

Now we can't do the volcano idea.

Luckily, Bethany had a really good new idea over the weekend too. You'll never guess what it is . . .

Elephant toothpaste!

It's easy squeezy peasy to make. Even easier than an exploding volcano! You just mix up four different kinds of special scientific stuff and pour it into a soft–drink bottle.

special science liquid

FOOD coloring

dishwashing liquid

yeast

And then . . . KA-POW! . . . this happens!

Lots of frothy, foamy foam grows and grows!

Now all we need is a giant toothbrush.

And some elephants! 😊😊😊

livia

One-Day-To-Go Tuesday

Only one more sleep before the big science fair!

Bethany brought in special badges for us all to wear. Bethany's really good at designing and drawing stuff. Even better than Ella!

Mr. Platt helped our class to make posters and banners for us to put up in our area of the auditorium.

Then all the groups did a quick practice of their experiments.

Ours is going to be super amazing! I really hope it works!!

☺livia

Science Fair Wednesday

Today was Science Fair Day!

We all set up our projects in the school auditorium. There were heaps of exciting things to see and do!

Lots of moms and dads and nannas and grandads came to see them as well. Mom came with Nanna Kate.

At eleven o'clock, Mr. Platt told our class to get our projects ready for the judges. They were going to decide which group would win the top prize!

Milo and Mehmet's group played their duck video on a special TV set. Everyone clapped when the experimenter wearing flippers won the race.

NO FLIPPERS

WITH FLIPPERS

Sage and Samira's rainbow looked beautiful.

And Jamila and Ivy's volcano went off with a BANG!

Finally, it was our group's turn. I felt like I had fluttery butterflies flitting around inside my tummy.

We all put on some special safety goggles. Daisy passed Bethany the first liquid. She poured it into the bottle. Then Nico poured another one in. Then Ava had a turn. Finally, I poured in the last ingredient. We held our breath.

Daisy   Bethany   OLIVIA   Ava

Harry   Matilda

Nico

Our elephant toothpaste started to grow!

It grew bigger
and bigger
and
bigger

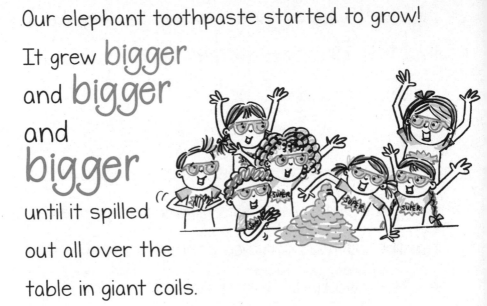

until it spilled
out all over the
table in giant coils.

Would it ever stop?
Would it take over
the school?

But after a few seconds it DID stop. Everybody clapped and cheered. Our experiment was **AMAZING!**

Matilda and I gave Bethany another squeezy group hug. ☺

livia

Cleanup Thursday

Our class spent the whole morning cleaning up our area in the auditorium. There were bits of glittery lava and elephant toothpaste everywhere!

Mr. Martini announced the winners of the science fair at a special assembly. The winner was . . .

a group from Grade 6.

But they deserved to win—they made a giant robot!

But guess what? The judges gave each grade a special award for effort. And the Super Science Stars won for our grade!

And guess what else? Bethany asked if
Matilda and I can come over to her house
this weekend. She's painting a big picture
on her garage wall and she wants us to
help.

It's going to be super fun!

I just hope she doesn't make us boiled
eggs for lunch! Pee-yew! ☺☺☺

livia

OLIVIA'S Secret Scribbles

Read them all!

OLIVIA'S Secret Scribbles — My NEW Best Friend

OLIVIA'S Secret Scribbles — My (Almost) Perfect Puppy

OLIVIA'S Secret Scribbles — AMAZING Acrobats

OLIVIA'S Secret Scribbles — The BIG CHICKEN Mystery

OLIVIA'S Secret Scribbles — Box Car Racers

OLIVIA'S Secret Scribbles — Super Science Stars